To the real Kiki
and her grandson Alex.
And to the love of my life.

Library of Congress Cataloging-in-Publication Data
Hanson, Warren.
   Kiki's Hats / written and illustrated by Warren Hanson.
      p. cm.
   Summary: Kiki loves to knit hats and give them away, leading many
   other people to be generous, as well.
   ISBN-13: 978-0-931674-94-5
   ISBN-10: 0-931674-94-8
   [1. Hats--Fiction. 2. Generosity--Fiction. 3. knitting--Fiction.
   4. Stories in rhyme.]   I. Title.
   PZ8.3.H19655kik 2007
   [E] --dc22   2007020524

TRISTAN Publishing, Inc.
2355 Louisiana Avenue North
Golden Valley, MN 55427

Please visit us at:
www.tristanpublishing.com

Kiki's Hats

written and illustrated by

Warren Hanson

TRISTAN PUBLISHING

Minneapolis

Kiki loved to sit and knit.
She knitted for the joy of it.
Summer, winter, fall and spring,
she sat there, knitting just one thing...

Hats.

Hats!

Hats!!

HATS!!

Ziggy, zaggy, stripey hats!

Brown hats,
white hats,
yellow,
red...

A heap of hats,
for any head.

A girl came by.

"Please, pardon me,
but do you sell these hats I see?"

"Oh, I don't make these hats for pay.
No, I make hats to give away!

You see that one that's green and blue?
I made that hat to give to you!"

The girl said,
"YAY!"
and ran right home,
her hat perched proudly
on her dome.

She soon returned to get another.

"May I have one for my brother?"

Kiki said, "Of course you may!
I made him this one, just today."

"Oh, thank you!" said the girl.
"And, please,
my friends would each LOVE one of these."

Then Kiki said,

"Here's what we'll do.

They can't have one... they must take TWO.

Keep one.

And give the other one.

Then come and tell me what you've done."

So each friend did as Kiki said.

They each put one hat on their head,

then ran away to have some fun
giving away the other one.

When they returned before too long,
their heads were bare!
Their hats were gone!

They said,
"We gave away each hat.
And it was FUN! Imagine that!"

"One hat is now a place to keep
new puppies cozy when they sleep."

"Another hat went to a man
asleep behind a garbage can."

"A family with lots of kids
now all have brand new knitted lids!"

"A girl whose house
went in a storm
now has a hat
to keep her warm."

"WHAT FUN!
Oh, EVERYONE should try it!"

Kiki raised her hand for quiet.

"I am proud of you for what you did with all your giving, but...
WHERE are the hats I gave to YOU?"

"We gave away our own hats, too!

We had such fun, we wondered...
may we have MORE hats to give away?"

"OH, YES!"

cried Kiki.

"Please, take some.
There's plenty more where those came from."

And it was true.
They all could see,
the pile had grown
impressively.

And yet, they stood there,
shuffling.
Then someone said,
"There's one more thing...

We hope you won't think this is wrong...
We... brought our Moms and Dads along.
THEY brought their bosses,
neighbors, brothers, doctors, teachers...
LOTS of others!

They LIKED what we got to do.
May they please give away some, too?"

"Oh, yes!"

"Oh, YES!"

"Oh, YES INDEED!"

cried Kiki.

"Please, take all you need!"

So everybody, old and young,
as if a starting bell had rung,
rushed forward with a loud

"HOORAY!"

and gathered hats to give away.

Then, as they started
to spread out,
behind them they heard
Kiki shout...

"Please remember,
everyone,
come back
and tell me
what you've
done!"

Soon postcards,

emails,

videos,

and photographs

arrived from those

who had received or given hats —

shepherds,

dancers,

diplomats,

grown-ups,

children,

rich and poor –

from far away
and right next door.

While Kiki's knitting needles twirled,
her hats went all around the world.

A hospital got hats to wear
for children there
who lose their hair.

A man who lives out on the street
now uses hats to warm his feet.

A blind boy in far-off Taiwan,
who giggled when he tried one on.

A man in coldest Kazakhstan
could not stay warm.
But now he can!

Soon, news reporters came,
with phones,
and cameras,
and microphones.

They called up to where Kiki sat,

"Please,
tell us all about
your hats."

"MY hats?" she laughed.
"They're not MY hats!
Now why on earth
would you think that?
These hats belong
to EVERYONE.
I only knit them,
just for fun.

If you want to find
news today,
take hats,
and give them
all away.
Then you'll find —
I know I'm right —
your stories
for the news
tonight."

Those news reporters did just that.
Each one picked out at least one hat,
then went and gave those hats away...

And yes, of course, needless to say,
they found their stories
(she was right!)
and showed them on the news that night.

Hats as prizes for good grades.

Hats for patients fighting AIDS.

Hats for schools and church bazaars.

For prison inmates behind bars.

Hats went out to nursing homes.

To bad hair people without combs!

Hats raised money for the poor...

and more, and more and more and more...

Wherever people needed care, Kiki's hats were given there.

Well, EVERYBODY saw the news.
And so they came –
in ones and twos,
and then in groups,
then crowds,
then SCADS!

The girl...
her friends...
their Moms and Dads...

Oh, people came from EVERYWHERE!

But Kiki,
well,
she wasn't there.

The hats
were all that
they could see –
a pile that climbed
eternally.

That heap of hats,
big as a mountain,
(numbering, if you'd
been counting,
FOURTEEN BILLION
SIXTY-SEVEN!)...

...had lifted Kiki right to heaven.

And there she's sitting, to this day,
still knitting hats to give away.

And all the people here below?
We know just what to do, you know.
It's up to each of us to do
the good that Kiki taught us to.
A helping hand.
Some time to share.
A little kindness here and there.
These are the hats WE give away,
and they keep giving, every day.

Our gifts live on and on.

And that's
the miracle of
Kiki's Hats.